Crystal Bowman is the author of the popular Jonathan James series for early readers as well as *Cracks in the Sidewalk* and *If Peas Could Taste Like Candy,* books of humorous poetry. She and her family live in Grand Rapids, Michigan.

Donna Christensen is an honors graduate of Kendall College of Art & Design in Grand Rapids, Michigan.

Mommy, May I Hug the Fishes?
Text copyright © 2000 by Crystal Bowman
Illustrations copyright © 2000 by Donna Christensen
Requests for information should be addressed to:

Zonder**kidz**

The Children's Group of ZondervanPublishingHouse
Grand Rapids, Michigan 49530
www.zonderkidz.com

Zonderkidz is a trademark of The Zondervan Corporation
ISBN: 0-310-23209-0

Art direction by Jody Langley
Design by Tobias Design, Grand Rapids

Printed in China

99 00 01 02 03 04 05 /v HK/ 10 9 8 7 6 5 4 3 2 1

Mommy, May I Hug the Fishes?

Written by Crystal Bowman

Illustrated by Donna Christensen

Zonderkidz

The Children's Group of ZondervanPublishingHouse

Mommy,

may I hug the fishes?
May I give them great
big kisses?

Mommy says,

"No, No, No!"

You may look,
but do not touch.
Fish don't like that
very much.

Mommy,

may I help you bake
a tummy-yummy
chocolate cake?

Mommy says,

"Yes,
Yes,
Yes!"

Here's a bowl for
you to mix
flour, milk, and
chocolate chips.

Mommy,

may I turn the knob?
May I turn the oven on?

Mommy says,

"NO, NO, NO!"
The oven's hot, you
could get burned.
That is something you
must learn.

Mommy,

may I play outside, take my teddy for a ride?

Mommy says,

"Yes,
Yes,
Yes!"

Ride and slide,
jump and play,
climb and run
outside today.

Mommy,

may I cross the
street
all by myself with
my two feet?

Mommy says,

"No, No, No!"

You might get lost or walk too far. You might not see a speeding car. No, you may not cross the street all by yourself with your two feet.

Mommy,

may I say a prayer?
Will God listen?
Does he care?

Mommy says,

"YES,

YES,

YES!"

Tell him what
you want to say.
He will listen
when you pray.

Mommy,

may I sing and clap,
Read a story in your
lap?

Mommy says,

"Yes, Yes, Yes!"

Let's read a book.
Let's sing and clap.
Snuggle and cuddle
in my lap.
Then you may take
a little nap.

Mommy says, "shh, shh, shh. . ."

Mom's Moment

As mothers, we want our children to enjoy the world around them. Because we love them, however, we set limits and say no to circumstances that are potentially harmful. God loves us as a mother loves her children (Isaiah 66:13). He wants us to enjoy the abundant life he offers us. But because he loves us, he also sets limits and says no to circumstances that are potentially harmful. Rest today in knowing that when your heavenly Father says no, he does so because he wants the best for you, his beloved child.